For Lawson—
      who led me to heaven's dancefloor…
and to Al—
      who didn't miss a beat.
          My love,
            Chara

I am dedicating this book to my wife, Regina, who encouraged me to make the journey of art, and to Chara for providing this vehicle to express it.
          Al

We wish to give special thanks to models Barbara ("Nanna") Saunders and Katherine Anne ("Little One") Carlson; Bob Saunders, who watches over us still; and Bruce Morrison for his generous support.
          Al and Chara

ILLUMINATION ARTS
PUBLISHING COMPANY, INC.
BELLEVUE, WASHINGTON

How Far To Heaven?

Words by Chara M. Curtis ❖ Paintings by Alfred Currier

ILLUMINATION ARTS
PUBLISHING COMPANY, INC.
BELLEVUE, WASHINGTON

I found Grandma on the porch swing, looking as though her mind were a million miles away. She was smiling, as she almost always does, and humming softly to herself. Not wanting to disturb her, I quietly turned away.

"Where are you going, Little One?" Her voice startled me.

"Oh, Nanna! I didn't think you could hear me."

Slowing the swing, she patted the seat beside her.

"Nanna is *always* listening for angels," she said.

What were you thinking about, Nanna?"

"To tell you the truth," she said, "I was just having a nice little chat with your grandpa."

"But, Nanna," I protested, "you said Grandpa is in *heaven!*"

"So he is, Little One." She gave my hand a squeeze. "So he is...."

As Nanna smiled into the distance, I wondered.

"Is heaven very far?" I finally asked.

"Let's go!" Nanna jumped up, her brown eyes sparkling. "Let's find out just how far it is!"

H and in hand, we walked through the gate into the lush green meadow beyond. At the very center, Nanna let go of my hand and plopped down flat on her back.

There she lay, arms outstretched, staring into the endless blue sky.

"Come join me," she grinned at my surprise.

Quietly we rested on our soft cushion of meadow grass, basking in the warmth of morning sun.

After a long lazy while, I felt her lightly nudge me.

"What are you thinking?" she asked.

"I'm pretending the whole sky is my blanket, and that's why I feel so safe and warm."

Nanna closed her eyes and drew a deep breath. She whispered, "Such a heavenly embrace!"

*A*lone feathery cloud drifted across the sky, and I watched as its wispy edges everflowed with new forms and faces.

I had a curious thought. "Nanna, do you think that clouds might really be people like Grandpa...just wearing different disguises while they watch us?"

Nanna stood up and blew a kiss toward the cloud.

"All things are possible in heaven."

The cloud slowly dwindled to but a few scattered feathers, gradually to fade and disappear. Yet I felt that from somewhere in that brilliant blue sky, someone was watching over me still.

ear the edge of the forest, Nanna stopped and cocked her head.

"Oh my!" she exclaimed. "How glorious! Do you hear it?"

"Hear what, Nanna?" All I heard was silence.

"The *orchestra*... the flutes and violins... why, even a piano!" She picked up a twig and waved it grandly through the air—like a symphony conductor with her baton.

I giggled when suddenly I recognized a sound.

"Oh, Nanna, those are just birds!"

"Precisely!" she beamed. "The orchestra."

anna reached out for me, and together we danced. Twirling and swirling, she sang:

"Wind sweeps through the trees like a violin's bow,
Rustling the leaves in boughs bended low.
Steady, the ribbitting rhythm of frogs
Echoes its tempo through hollowed-out logs.
The many-voiced brook as it babbles along
Is ever creating new words to the song.
All Nature resounds the divine symphony,
And upon the great stage, the dancer is me!"

We danced and danced, whirling dizzily around until we fell laughing onto the soft forest floor. Then, clutching the ground, we giggled and moaned as the trees spun around us in a whirr.

"Oh, Nanna," I cried, "I've never heard such beautiful music!"

"This music," she smiled, "is one of heaven's voices. Come, we must be getting very close!"

*O*ur footsteps slowed with the arrival of a delicious new fragrance.

"What is this *wonderful* smell, Nanna?"

She inhaled deeply, eyes wide with delight. "I've heard the air in heaven smells of sweet perfume! You don't suppose we've arrived, do you?"

We raced down the trail until…there it was, a magnificent thicket of wild roses.

"Oh my!" Nanna exclaimed, pressing her nose to the petals.

I carefully picked a rose — the prettiest one I could reach — and gave it to her with a kiss.

As Nanna placed the flower in her silvery hair, a small teardrop rolled from her eye.

"Oh, thank you," she whispered, returning my kiss. "Surely heaven is but one breath away."

W e continued our journey playfully, splashing in pools of sunlight that spilled through the trees.

Nanna paused to gaze down the radiant path ahead.

"I am told the streets of heaven are bathed in streams of gold," she said.

Now as we walked through the gleaming treasure, I felt like the richest person on Earth!

*T*he path led to the edge of Singing Rock Stream, where Nanna quickly slipped off her shoes. We dangled our toes in the cool, sparkling water and watched the ripples dance in everwidening circles.

"Do you hear the music, Nanna?"

"Oh, yes," she sighed. "It's so lovely."

"And the smell?"

"It is of sweet perfume!" She nodded and lovingly touched her rose.

A tickly-soft feeling fluttered inside me, as though my heart had grown wings.

"You know what, Nanna? Sometimes I feel like I could fly!"

She looked into my eyes and gently brushed my cheek.

"Grandpa said that in heaven an angel would be at my side. Do you not know you are my angel?"

The sun glistened gold on the crystal-clear water…upstream and down, without end. I took Nanna's hands and we danced to the music. I can still hear her singing as then:

"Forever and always, inside, all around,
Heaven is everywhere heaven is found.
Listen with glad ears, see with love's eyes,
Give wings to your heart, and cherish the prize!
Forever and always we dance to the sound,
For heaven is everywhere heaven is found."

Chara M. Curtis writes for her own entertainment and enjoyment. "I really should get out more, but I take such fantastic journeys in my mind!" *How Far to Heaven?* is one example.

Author of *All I See Is Part Of Me* and *Fun Is A Feeling*, Chara makes her home in the Pacific Northwest, where she says, "I try to keep as busy as the sky."

Alfred Currier is primarily a plein-air painter. He prefers responding to his subjects personally, while immersed in the spirit of the moment. His paintings for *How Far To Heaven?* are an exception, reflecting his style of conceptual inspiration.

Al received his formal training at the Columbus College of Art and Design and the American Academy of Art in Chicago, where he earned his degree in fine art. He makes his home in Anacortes, Washington.

Look for
All I See Is Part Of Me and ***Fun Is A Feeling***
also from ILLUMINATION ARTS
written by Chara M. Curtis.

Book Design by Molly Murrah
Typography by Typography, Ltd.

Published in The United States of America.
Printed by Tien Wah Press of Singapore.

Publisher's Cataloging in Publication
(Prepared by Quality Books Inc.)

Curtis, Chara M.
 How far to heaven? / words by Chara M. Curtis; paintings by Alfred Currier.
 p. cm.
 SUMMARY: A young girl and her grandmother explore the beauty and wonder of nature
in the woods behind their house, looking for the answer to the question "Is heaven very far?"
 Preassigned LCCN: 93-1918.
 ISBN 0-935699-06-6

 1. Metaphysics—Juvenile fiction.   I. Currier, Alfred, ill.   II. Title.
PZ7.C878Ix 1993   [Fic]
                                           QBI93-1073

ILLUMINATION ARTS
PUBLISHING COMPANY, INC.
P.O. BOX 1865
BELLEVUE, WA 98009